T0724296

Ginger and Alice

by
John Hyland

This publication contains the opinions and ideas of its author. It is intended to provide helpful and informative material on the subjects addressed in the publication. The author and publisher specifically disclaim all responsibility for any liability, loss or risk, personal or otherwise, which is incurred as a consequence, directly or indirectly, of the use and application of any of the contents of this book.

WORKBOOK PRESS LLC
187 E Warm Springs Rd,
Suite B285, Las Vegas, NV 89119, USA

Website: https://workbookpress.com/
Hotline: 1-888-818-4856
Email: admin@workbookpress.com

Ordering Information:
Quantity sales. Special discounts are available on quantity purchases by corporations, associations, and others.
For details, contact the publisher at the address above.

ISBN-13:   978-1-953839-07-7 (Paperback Version)
                978-1-953839-08-4 (Digital Version)

REV. DATE: 27/10/2020

CHAPTER 1

Ginger the gerbil had never been more frightened than the day she found herself trapped in that awful box. The box was so small she barely had room to turn around in it. The only light she could see came through a few tiny holes in its sides.

To make matters worse, the box tipped back and forth. Once it even turned upside down! Ginger's heart beat wildly as she scrambled to stay on her feet.

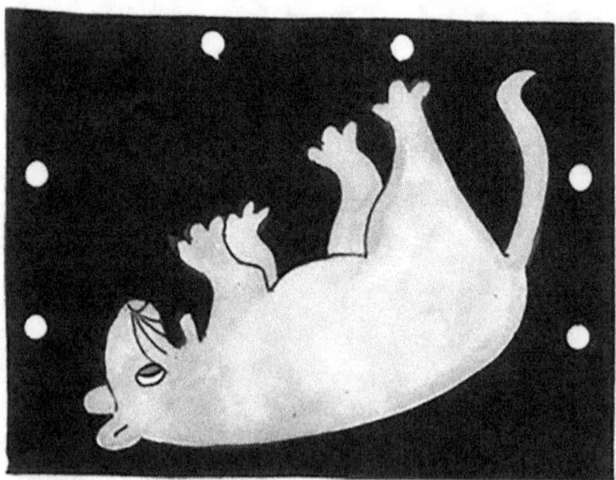

"What's going to happen to me?" she wondered. She would have given anything to be back in Mr. Green's pet store.

Outside the box two people were talking. "Billy!" Mrs. Franklin exclaimed. "Hold that box still or you'll hurt your little gerbil. You're making me so nervous I'm having trouble driving."

"But I'm excited, Mom," Billy replied. "I can't wait to see how Ginger likes Alice!"

Ginger knew who the Franklins were because they had bought her from Mr. Green half an hour ago. Now they were taking her somewhere and talking about someone named Alice.

"Alice must live with Billy and his mother," Ginger thought. "I'm supposed to like her, so I hope she's friendly!"

Gradually the box stopped moving. Ginger was still upset, however, and her nose twitched nervously. Pulling her tail up close to her body, she crouched in the darkness and waited.

Ginger was unhappy because she didn't know who Alice was, but she also missed two gerbils named Spice and Fluff, who had lived with her in Mr. Green's pet store. She remembered all the fun she'd had with them, running in an exercise wheel in the corner of their cage.

The three gerbils had held contests in the wheel to see who could run the fastest and the longest. Ginger had won nearly every time, leaving Spice and Fluff huffing and puffing to catch their breath.

"You guys are just too fat," Ginger joked. "Better stop eating so much." "It's not our fault," Spice laughed. "We can't resist all the delicious sunflower and squash seeds Mr. Green feeds us." "Then there's that tasty wheat and barley," said Fluff. "We can't let so much good food go to waste!"

Life in the pet store had been pleasant until half an hour ago. Ginger had just eaten a plump sunflower seed when she noticed Billy watching her. "Let's buy that gerbil!" he called to his mother, who was standing behind him.

"Which one?" she asked.

"That brown one," Billy replied, pointing at Ginger.

Before Ginger realized what was happening, Mr. Green had reached into the cage and caught her by the tail. Then he had lifted her out of the cage and lowered her carefully into his other hand.

"This may look like a bad way to handle gerbils," Mr. Green had explained. "But it doesn't hurt them a bit. They don't get as frightened as when someone grabs them around the body and picks them up."

Ginger had felt comfortable in Mr. Green's hand because he had stroked her back and talked gently to her. But then he had put her into that awful box! Mr. Green had said Ginger would be all right because the box had air holes, but he hadn't mentioned how small and dark it was.

Billy had carried the box out of the store to the family car, and now Ginger was traveling to meet some mysterious person named Alice. It was all very disturbing!

CHAPTER 2

Ginger thought the trip would never end. She was able to rest after Billy's mother made him hold the box still, but her legs and back were getting cramped. If she just had room to stretch, she'd feel much better. She wondered how much longer it would be before she got out of the box. "And where will I be when I'm outside?" she asked herself.

Suddenly the box started swaying again, and Ginger heard Billy's mother tell him to be careful when he carried it to the house. A car door opened and slammed shut. The box bounced wildly for a few seconds, another door opened and closed, and Ginger felt a jolt beneath her feet. The box was motionless now, resting on some hard, level surface.

A crack of light appeared above Ginger. Looking up, she saw Billy's hand reaching down toward her. "Come on, Ginger; we're home!" he exclaimed. "It's time for you to make friends with Alice."

Billy quickly lifted Ginger from the box by the tail, but he was so excited he almost dropped her.

"Take it easy, son!" his mother laughed. "You want Ginger to be in one piece when she meets Alice."

As Ginger dangled from Billy's hand, she caught a glimpse of a large room filled with furniture. She didn't get a good look, however, because Billy quickly lowered her into a huge glass-sided container.

The bottom of the container was covered with a thick layer of soft, clean wood shavings. In one corner stood an exercise wheel. A food bowl had been placed beside the wheel. Above the bowl on the side of the container hung a water bottle.

"This looks a lot like our cage in the pet store, only a lot bigger," Ginger thought. But when she turned around, she was startled by a most unusual sight.

It was a miniature two-story mansion! It was long and blue and had six upstairs and downstairs windows, each with red shutters. A porch with a green railing ran along the front of the house, and a bright yellow door formed its main entrance. Directly above this door was a smaller purple door with a pink balcony. The mansion had a purple roof that peaked just beneath a screen covering the container.

"Whoever lives here must be really important – or really strange," thought Ginger.

"This is Alice's house," said Billy, leaning over the container. "She's inside sleeping, as usual. Let's wake her up."

Billy tapped on the roof. When nothing happened, he

shook the house. After a few seconds the yellow door opened and a furry head appeared. Then a plump gray gerbil came out and stretched lazily on the porch beneath the balcony.

Ginger was nervous, but she stepped forward and spoke as calmly as she could. "I'm very pleased to meet you, Alice. I'm really glad you're a gerbil. I had no idea **what** you'd be!"

Alice looked at Ginger with a haughty expression. "**Of course** I'm a gerbil! What did you expect? A frog or a lizard?"

"What I meant is that I'm happy to see you're just like me," Ginger explained.

"Well, maybe not just like you," sniffed Alice. "I'll bet you never lived in a big fancy house like mine, and I don't suppose you get petted every day. Do you always have squash seeds and the best peanuts and pistachios to eat? Not every gerbil does, you know!"

Ginger felt uncomfortable, but she did her best to make a good impression. "Can't we be friends?" she asked. "I'd like that very much."

"I guess we can **try** to get along," sighed Alice. "The Franklins must think you'll be good for me, but we'll have to wait to find out. By the way, what's your name?"

"Ginger."

"Hmmm. I've heard worse names and I've heard better names, so I guess yours will do. Where'd you come from?"

Ginger told Alice that she'd lived in Mr. Green's pet store for as long as she could remember. She also described all of the fun she'd had with Spice and Fluff.

"We ran a lot in an exercise wheel," Ginger explained. "Say, you've got a wheel here, too! We could have contests to see who can run the fastest and the longest."

Alice had burrowed into the thick wood shavings in front of her house until only her head was visible. When Ginger suggested they use the exercise wheel, she yawned and said, "Oh, dear, no. I have much more important things to do." "But don't you get exercise?" Ginger asked "Of course I do," snapped Alice. "I've got six rooms to take care of in my mansion. Try to imagine all the wood shavings I have to carry in to make them as comfortable as possible. Then I have to chew away the edges of the doors. For some reason they're getting so small I barely have room to squeeze through!"

Ginger suspected that Alice was getting too fat for her house but didn't want to say so and make her angry. Instead, she asked Alice what she did to have fun.

"I play all kinds of tricks on the Franklins. **I'm an expert mischief maker.**"

"But how can you do that?" asked Ginger. "Don't the Franklins keep you in here all the time? You'd have to get out to make mischief, and I've noticed there's a screen over the top of the container."

Alice scratched her ear with her hind foot and sat up. "I escape whenever I want," she declared. "Billy takes me out at least three times every day to play. If he holds me too loosely, I jump to the floor and scamper under a chair or the sofa. I also get out by climbing up on the roof of my house and squeezing under the screen. Either way, I create a lot of excitement."

"What kind of excitement?" asked Ginger.

"I'll let you know in a minute," said Alice. "Right now I need a snack. Talking takes energy, you know."

Alice invited Ginger to join her, and soon they were munching squash seeds, peanuts and pistachios from the bowl near the exercise wheel. Ginger was so eager to hear about Alice's tricks that she ate very little. Alice stuffed herself, however.

Soon she was lying on her back with her front paws resting on her bulging stomach. Then she continued her explanation.

"When I get loose, I often chew things," Alice declared. "Once I gnawed a hole through the living room rug right in front of the television set. That really made Mrs. Franklin angry!"

Alice smiled proudly, then continued her story. "Another time Mr. Franklin was relaxing in his easy chair with a newspaper. When he fell asleep, I climbed up on his chest and chewed up the page he'd been reading. Then two days ago I bit through the tube that bubbles air through the water in Billy's tropical fish tank. By the time he discovered the air was off, all of the fish were gasping for oxygen."

"That was a pretty mean thing to do," said Ginger, feeling sorry for the fish.

"Well, I guess it was kind of cruel," Alice admitted, "but some of my tricks are really funny. Last Thursday afternoon I hid between the cushions on the sofa just before Mrs. Larson and Mrs. Peterson came over to visit Mrs. Franklin. When Mrs. Peterson sat down on the sofa, I popped up right beside her. She screamed and jumped up on a chair."

"How are you able to do all those crazy things?" Ginger asked in amazement. "Can't the Franklins catch you when you get loose?"

"Not very easily," boasted Alice. "I may be a little out of shape, but I'm really quite nimble. Besides, I'm small enough to hide in odd places. Just before Christmas last year I spent half a day sleeping among the presents beneath the tree. No one would have found me if I hadn't gotten hungry and come out. I let Billy put me back in the container so I could eat the walnuts and almonds and filberts he'd given me as a holiday treat."

Ginger looked puzzled. "But if you do so many things that upset the Franklins, don't they punish you?"

Alice smiled and combed her whiskers with her front paws. "That's the best part of it," she laughed. "Whenever they catch me – or whenever I let myself get caught – I look as sad as I can. They say I'm s-o-o cute and forgive me. They like me so much they give me everything, as you can see by looking at my mansion."

"You're really lucky!" said Ginger.

Alice had finished combing her whiskers and was now grooming her tail. "I'm not as lucky as you think," she sighed. "Sometimes the Franklins go too far. For instance, they thought I was lonely and went out and bought you to live with me. Can you imagine that? I'm so busy I don't have time to get lonesome."

"But everyone needs somebody to talk to and do things with," replied Ginger, remembering the wonderful times she had with Spice and Fluff in the pet store. "Don't you suppose we could be happy together?"

Alice wrinkled her forehead. "Well, that's something I'll have to think about. I'm pretty independent. But we may be able to get along if you can learn to enjoy being pampered by the Franklins. You'll also have to get used to **all the weird clown pictures in the house.** They're on everything – on furniture and dishes and even on the clothes Billy and his mother wear. And, of course, I'll expect you to help me when I get out and make mischief."

"I'll do my best," Ginger promised. "Then maybe you can run in the exercise wheel with me. If you do that every day, the doors in your mansion should stop getting smaller."

"I can't imagine how that could happen," snorted Alice. "But we can talk about it later. Let's get some rest now. You must be worn out from your ride from the pet store. I could use a nap myself. Talking wears a person out, you know."

Alice took Ginger into her mansion, showed her every room, and told her she could sleep wherever she wanted. Ginger chose a room upstairs that had a window with pink lace curtains. As she curled up and closed her eyes, she wondered what her new life with Alice would be like.

"It won't be like living in the pet store," she thought. "But it sure should be interesting!"

CHAPTER 3

Ginger slept soundly and woke up well rested, but she thought she'd been dreaming about a fat gray gerbil who lived in a fancy house. Until she opened her eyes, she believed she was still in Mr. Green's pet store. "Wait until I tell Fluff and Spice about my crazy dream," she chuckled. "They'll really laugh!"

Ginger was surprised to see the window with pink curtains. Just then, Alice poked her head into the room. "Well, are you ready to start making mischief?" she asked. "We've both had a good rest, so we should be able to play some really neat tricks on the Franklins."

Alice's sudden appearance startled Ginger. "I-I guess I'm ready," she stammered. "But we won't get into serious trouble, will we?" "Don't worry," said Alice. "I know how to play the right kind of tricks. Didn't I tell you I'm an expert mischief maker?"

Ginger wasn't sure she could trust Alice's judgment because she remembered her story about cutting off air to Billy's fish. She didn't want to argue, however, so she decided to wait and see what happened.

"OK!" Alice declared. "Let's get going. Since you've never made mischief before, we'll keep things simple by crawling under the screen over the container. We could jump out of Billy's hand when he takes us out to play, but it takes a lot of practice to escape like that."

The two gerbils climbed to the roof of the mansion. Then after making sure no one was watching, they squeezed under the screen.

"That was easy enough," Ginger said to herself. But when

she looked down at the table on which the container was standing, she got frightened. "How are we going to get down from here?" she asked Alice. "We'll have to drop almost two feet, and that's a long way!"

"Just watch me," Alice answered. Gripping the edge of the container with her front paws, she lowered herself down the outside. Then she let go and landed on her plump bottom on the table. "See, there's nothing to it," she laughed, bouncing to her feet.

"It may be nothing for someone like you who's so well padded, but I might break my neck!" thought Ginger as she prepared to drop. "Don't be afraid," called Alice. "I'll catch you."

Ginger released her grip and immediately found herself sprawled across Alice. "Ahem!" Alice complained. "You definitely have to work on your landing! But don't worry about that now. Let's get off the table. Slide down the leg like this."

In a few seconds Alice and Ginger were standing on the living room floor, ready for adventure. "Follow me!" Alice ordered.

The two gerbils scurried into the kitchen. As Ginger hurried to keep up, her feet slipped on the smooth tile floor. Skidding forward, she crashed into Alice, who had stopped beside a wastebasket at the top of the basement stairs.

"You've got to be more careful if you expect to make mischief right," scolded Alice. "Now pay attention because this is really important!"

As Ginger watched, Alice nudged the basket with her nose. "Good!" she exclaimed. "It's not heavy, so we can push it down the stairs and let the Franklins know we're out. Then they'll try to catch us while we're playing other tricks."

Ginger wasn't sure Alice's plan made sense. "Wouldn't it be easier to make mischief if no one chased us?" she asked.

"Of course it would," replied Alice impatiently. "But that wouldn't be any challenge for me. All expert mischief makers do their best when people try to stop them from playing tricks. Now do exactly as I do." Alice put her front paws against the side of the basket, and so did Ginger.

"Push!" cried Alice. The basket tipped forward slowly. "Push harder!"

Puffing and straining, the two gerbils sent the wastebasket clattering down the basement stairs. A moment later, Mrs. Franklin called from somewhere beyond the living room.

"Billy! Where are you?"

"In here, Mom," shouted Billy. "In my bedroom."

"Then who's making all that noise in the kitchen?" The thump of running feet echoed through the house.

"What do we do now?" asked Ginger. "We get out of here, of course," said Alice. "I'll show you how to escape."

Alice darted back through the kitchen with Ginger close behind. The thumping was louder now. As the two gerbils dashed into the living room, they saw two pairs of feet rushing toward them. "It's Alice!" Mrs. Franklin exclaimed. "And Ginger's with her. Catch them, Billy!"

Billy dove to the floor and grabbed for his two pets. He missed and grabbed again, but Alice and Ginger ducked behind a china cabinet a half second before he could reach them.

"Whew! That was close!" Alice panted. "Either Billy's getting faster or I'm getting slower."

"I can't breathe!" gasped Ginger.

"You're just a bit rattled," Alice told her. "Rest here while I run over to that palm tree in the pot by the closet door. Billy and his mother are looking for us on the other side of the china cabinet, so I don't think they'll see me."

"What are you going to do to the tree?" asked Ginger, sounding worried.

Alice laughed and said, "I'm going to loosen the soil a little so it can grow better."

Before Ginger could say anything more, Alice was off.

Keeping close to the wall, she ran to the pot and jumped up into it. A second later she was digging furiously at the base of the tree. A shower of dirt flew onto the floor. Turning around, Alice sent another shower in the opposite direction.

"Why, you little rascal!" screamed Mrs. Franklin when she saw the flying dirt. "I just vacuumed the rug this morning!" Billy sprinted toward the palm tree, but Alice had already leaped from the pot and disappeared beneath the sofa.

Mrs. Franklin threw up her hands in disgust and said, "Of all the places that pesky gerbil could hide, she had to pick the sofa! If she climbs up into the springs, we may never get her out."

Mrs. Franklin pulled the cushions from the sofa and tossed them on the floor. "We won't be able to see anything without a flashlight," she told Billy. "Get the one from the drawer by the refrigerator."

Billy shined the light down into the springs. "Hey Mom!" he exclaimed. "Here's that water pistol I lost last summer, and there's Dad's extra set of car keys. He's been looking for them for two days."

"But do you see Alice?" asked Mrs. Franklin. "Not yet," Billy replied.

"Keep looking, son. She's got to be in there somewhere."

Billy and his mother were so busy searching the sofa that they didn't see Alice scamper back to Ginger behind the china cabinet. "I really fooled those two," she boasted."You did make them look pretty foolish," Ginger agreed. "But what's next?"

"Now we're going to make some super mischief!" declared

Alice. "You'll really like this trick. I'm going to surprise you."

Alice peeped from behind the cabinet to check on Billy and his mother. They were on their hands and knees now, looking under the sofa.

The two gerbils scrambled under one side of Mr. Franklin's big easy chair, which stood beside the living room window. "Keep going until we come out on the other side," ordered Alice. "OK. Now tell me what you see."

"I see a table," Ginger replied.

"Notice that fancy doily hanging over the edge," said Alice. "If I stand on your back and reach way up, I can grab it and pull it off the table. Then we'll really have some excitement!"

"What's so exciting about pulling a doily off of a table?" asked Ginger, thinking Alice had no imagination.

"It isn't the doily that's going to cause the excitement," Alice replied. "It's Mrs. Franklin's fancy glass vase that's standing on the doily."

"Yikes!" cried Ginger. "We'll get into really serious trouble! The vase will break into a million pieces, and we'll be smashed flat."

"Don't be silly," Alice laughed. "Didn't I tell you the Franklins never get really angry with me because I'm so cute? And we won't be hurt because we'll jump out of the way at the last second."

Ginger didn't like Alice's plan, but before she could reply, Alice was climbing on her back and eyeing the doily. "Ooof! She must weigh a ton," gasped Ginger.

Alice stretched as high as she could and just managed to grab the doily. Then she tugged as hard as she could. "That vase is heavier than I thought," she grunted. "I can't seem to move it!"

"You could let go, and we could play some other kind of mischief that wouldn't cause any damage," Ginger wheezed.

"No way!" snapped Alice. "Remember what I said about experts doing their best under pressure? Well, this is one of those times. I'm not going to give up!"

The doily inched downward. Soon the vase could be seen teetering on the edge of the table.

"Get ready to jump aside because I'm going to give it one more big yank!" cried Alice.

"No you won't!" said an angry voice from behind. Ginger and Alice felt Billy grab their tails, and the next instant they were hanging upside down.

"You should be ashamed of yourselves!" Billy scolded as he held the two gerbils suspended, one in each hand. "Pushing the wastebasket down the stairs was funny, and we can forgive you for getting the rug dirty. But you should never have tried to break Mom's favorite vase! If we'd known you were planning to do that, we wouldn't have given you the cake."

"What cake?" wondered Ginger, as Billy put her and Alice back into the container. She didn't have to wonder long, however, because there sat the cake on the porch of Alice's mansion, decorated with pink frosting and blue candy flowers.

"We really should be ashamed of ourselves," cried Ginger. "The Franklins have given us a special treat, and we've really upset them!"

Alice had already bitten into the cake. "Not to worry," she mumbled with her mouth full of frosting. "The Franklins won't stay angry long. They'll soon forget we tried to smash the vase. Then everything will be back to normal."

"Don't be so sure," warned Ginger, looking up at the top of the container. "Billy just laid a thick, heavy book across the screen, and now he's taping the screen down. I'm afraid we're prisoners!"

"That doesn't mean anything," laughed Alice, gobbling a candy flower. "Billy will be playing with us before you know it. Now quit talking and have some of this yummy stuff before I eat it all!"

CHAPTER 4

Ginger tried the cake. It was delicious, but she felt uncomfortable. "I'm not sure we should be eating this," she told Alice. "All the books about gerbils in Mr. Green's pet store say our main food is seeds and grains. Bits of apples and lettuce are also good for us. We can even eat dried dog and cat food now and then. But there's nothing in the books about cake."

Alice licked the last bit of frosting from her whiskers. "All of those writers are humans," she replied with a smirk. "They have no idea what's really good for us gerbils. Now, if I wrote those books, it'd be different. I'd explain how we love cake and candy and ice cream and everything else that's sweet. Maybe someday when I'm not so busy making mischief, I'll become an author and tell the true story."

"You could also let everybody know you're an expert at playing **harmless** tricks," complained Ginger. She was still upset about the vase they had almost smashed.

"I'll tell them that, too!" bragged Alice, without realizing what Ginger really meant. "Everyone loves to read about expert mischief makers."

Ginger was beginning to suspect that Alice was hopelessly self centered, but she didn't think it would do any good to tell her. Instead, she asked what Alice planned to do, now that Billy had taped and weighted down the screen over the container.

Alice yawned and said she intended to rest until the Franklins got over being angry. "It won't be long," she assured Ginger. "I just hope I have time for a good snooze before Billy comes back and wants to play. You'd better get some shut-eye, too."

Ginger was weary from her adventures on the kitchen and living room floor, so she went into the mansion with Alice and slept for two hours. When the two gerbils awoke, they came out and looked up at the top of the container. The book still lay across the screen. The tape was still there, too, and there was no sign of Billy.

"We may never get out of here," moaned Ginger. "I hope the Franklins at least come back to feed us!"

"There's no need to worry," Alice replied. "Billy and his mother are probably out shopping. Or maybe they went to see his grandmother. By the way, did I tell you what I did once when Grams came and stayed overnight? I snuck into bed with her and scared her half to death.""You may not be able to play those awful tricks again," Ginger replied. "I think the Franklins are fed up with your nonsense."

"Nonsense?" exclaimed Alice. "Weren't you listening when I explained how important mischief making is?"

"All I know is that Billy and his mother are angry with us, and I can't say I blame them," said Ginger.

"Well, go ahead and be an old grump," replied Alice, getting testy. "You won't see **me** getting upset!"

Alice sat down on the porch of the mansion, leaned back against the railing, and began humming "Happy Days Are Here Again." Then she combed her whiskers and tail, smoothed down the fur on her stomach, and smiled. She certainly looked relaxed.

In a few minutes, however, Alice began to fidget. She was still sitting on the porch, but now she was jerking her left foot up and down and whistling "Nobody Knows the

Trouble I've Seen." Soon she was burrowing like a mad mole back and forth beneath the thick wood shavings in front of the mansion. When she had finished her sixth tunnel, she popped up beside the food bowl, picked up a delicious pistachio, then dropped it uneaten.

"This is really serious!" said Ginger to herself. "Alice without an appetite is like a fish without fins and scales. She's definitely upset."

At that moment two cheerful voices called out "Hi, guys!" Looking up, Ginger and Alice saw Billy and Mrs. Franklin removing the book and tape from the screen.

"Didn't I tell you to stay calm?" cried Alice, trying not to sound excited. "I knew all along that things would soon be back to normal because I know exactly how Billy and his mother think!" "Things may be back to normal," Ginger replied. "But I'm not sure you knew it all along."

Alice would have argued that point, but Billy was talking now. "Mom and I have been shopping, and guess what? We have something special for both of you."

"I hope it's another cake," exclaimed Alice. "I could eat one all by myself right now!"

As Mrs. Franklin watched, Billy held out two miniature vests. "How do you guys like these?" he asked. "The red one with the big yellow dots is for you, Alice. Ginger gets the one with the blue and white stripes. Mom and I had to go to five different pet stores before we found them. They cost six dollars apiece, but we knew you guys needed them."

Alice scowled and ground her teeth. "That's ridiculous," she snorted. "Whoever heard of gerbils needing clothes? This time the Franklins have really gone too far!"

"I don't think those are just clothes," said Ginger. "They have funny looking rings on the back of them."

"Well, whatever they are, you won't catch me wearing anything that stupid!" Alice insisted. "I'd rather kiss a frog."

Before Alice and Ginger could say anything more, Billy and Mrs. Franklin grabbed their tails and lifted them from the container. Working quickly, they stuck Alice's and Ginger's front legs through the arm holes in the vests. Next, they closed two strong snaps that held the vests in place in front. Billy hooked a long, thin chain to the ring on each vest. Then he and Mrs. Franklin set the two gerbils down on the living room floor beside a coffee table.

"We don't like to treat you two like prisoners, but you're getting too mischievous," said Mrs. Franklin. "We can put up with most of your tricks, but we can't let you break things."

Alice looked as sad as she could, expecting sympathy.

Mrs. Franklin wasn't impressed. "You've fooled us with that cute look before, but it won't work now. This time we have to punish you."

Mrs. Franklin told Alice and Ginger that Billy would play with them every day. However, they would have to wear their vests whenever he took them out of the container. "The chains on the vests will keep you from getting away when you're out," Billy added. "I'll hook the other ends to the coffee table, like this."

Ginger and Alice walked the length of their chains. They found they had plenty of room to move around, but they also discovered that the palm tree and the table with the vase were well out of reach. Everything else that might be damaged had been removed to a safe distance, too.

"Clever; very clever," said Alice with a smile. "I had no

idea the Franklins were so smart."

"Aren't you angry?" asked Ginger, hardly believing what she'd just heard. "You said you'd rather kiss a frog than wear that vest!"

"I still feel that way," Alice replied.

Ginger rubbed her eyes to make sure they were working properly. "Then why are you smiling?" she asked. "You realize your mischief-making days are over, don't you?"

"Oh, no they're not," Alice chuckled. "We've got to get rid of these dumb vests before we can play tricks again, but that shouldn't be too much trouble for someone with my brains. I'm looking forward to the challenge."

"What exactly will you do?" asked Ginger, completely puzzled.

"I'm not sure, but I'll think of something soon," Alice promised.

The two gerbils felt a tug on their chains. It was Mrs. Franklin trying to get their attention. "Billy and I want you to understand we're sorry we have to punish you this way," she said. "And we want you to know you'll only have to wear your vests and chains until you learn to behave."

"That's it!" whispered Alice to Ginger. "I've just thought of a perfect plan for outsmarting the Franklins. But don't ask me to explain. You'll be able to tell soon just by watching me."

CHAPTER 5

Ginger watched Alice carefully but couldn't discover her plan. After a week she became upset because Alice seemed perfectly content to wear her vest and be chained to the coffee table. To make matters worse, Alice didn't seem to mind playing ridiculous games with Billy.

"I can't believe you had fun today," Ginger complained one afternoon as she and Alice munched peanuts from their seed bowl. "Do you know how silly you looked this morning wearing that cowboy outfit and riding that cardboard horse?"

"Well, what do you think **you** looked like riding up and down on Billy's tinker-toy ferris wheel?" snapped Alice.

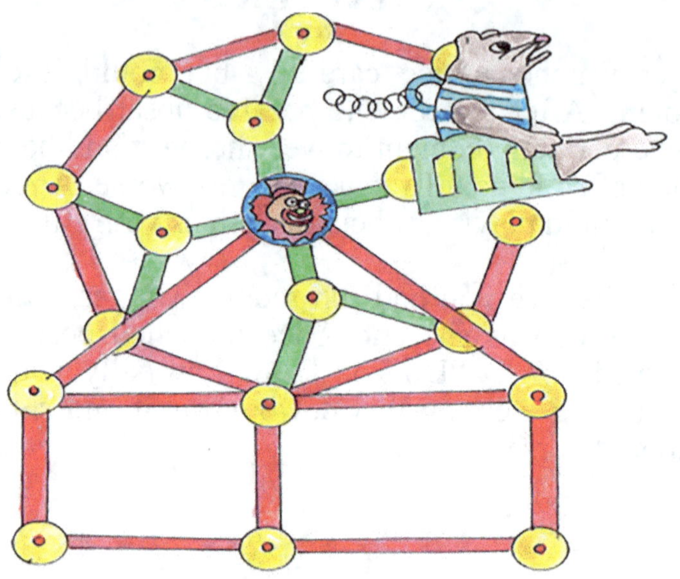

"And why do you let Billy tie that little plastic truck to your tail so you can pull it around?"

"I've got no way of escaping from my vest and chain,"

Ginger sighed. "But you said you had a plan for outsmarting the Franklins. Why don't you use it?"

"I can't believe you're so dense!" laughed Alice. "Don't you realize I'm fooling the Franklins right now? They think I'm learning to behave, so they'll let me loose soon. Then they'll really be surprised when I run wild and make all kinds of super mischief! And when other people find out about my tricks, I'll be famous."

Ginger slapped her forehead with her paw and wondered how she could have made such a silly mistake. "I-I didn't understand your plan because I didn't think it was so simple," she explained. "I thought you might do something complicated like going on a diet until you were thin enough to slip out of your vest. And for all I knew, you might have been planning to escape by gnawing through the coffee table when Billy wasn't watching."

Alice shook her head. "The diet wouldn't have worked because I would have been too weak to move by the time I was thin enough to escape. But I like the idea of chewing through the table. Why didn't you suggest it before I started pretending to be good?"

"It doesn't matter what you do," Ginger replied, getting disgusted. "If you make serious trouble after the Franklins let you loose, they'll just find some other way to punish you. And it might be a lot worse than being chained up!"

Alice waved her paw impatiently. "That will never happen!" she insisted. "Billy and his mother and father will be so impressed by my new tricks that they'll never want to control me again!"

"Well, don't expect me to help," Ginger declared. "When I get rid of my vest and chain, I'll never cause any more trouble!"

"Then you can just forget about becoming famous like me!" exclaimed Alice in an angry voice. "And to think I wasted so much time trying to teach you to create excitement with wastebaskets, palm trees and doilies!"

Alice was so angry she wouldn't speak to Ginger the rest of the day. The thought of losing Alice's friendship worried Ginger more than the fear of getting into trouble with the Franklins, so she told Alice she might help her again if she promised not to ruin anything.

"You can do whatever you want, but I'm moving up to heavy-duty mischief," snorted Alice. "Things will get really exciting once I get started."

Alice said she expected to begin making new mischief soon because the Franklins were almost convinced she had learned to behave. Her prediction seemed about to come true two days later when Mrs. Franklin appeared with a big dish of maple nut ice cream. As she set the dish on the porch of Alice's mansion, she praised both gerbils for playing so well with Billy.

"You guys won't be wearing those vests and chains much longer," she promised. "But before we take them off for good, we have to make sure you can control yourselves. If you can get along with Eenee and Meenee for just one week, you'll be free. I'll introduce you to them after you've finished your treat."

"Who can Eenee and Meenee be?" Ginger wondered. "With names like that, they may not be very nice."

Alice couldn't answer because her mouth was filled with ice cream. When she was able to speak, she laughed. "If they were named Sluggo and Spike they might be dangerous, but Eenee and Meenee are sissy names. We've got nothing to worry about!"

After the two gerbils had eaten their fill, Billy put their vests on them and set them on the living room floor.

"Here comes Mom with your new playmates," he said as he hooked their chains to the coffee table. Mrs. Franklin was carrying two small parrots, one perched on each hand. Both of them had bright green bodies and bright yellow heads. As she held them out toward Ginger and Alice, they bobbed their heads and screeched.

"Eenee and Meenee are delighted to see you," Mrs. Franklin explained. "They're full of pep, so you guys shouldn't get bored playing with them."

Ginger looked puzzled. "How're we supposed to tell them apart? They look and act exactly alike, and they certainly sound the same."

"Why do you think they're named Eenee and Meenee?" growled Alice, clapping her paws over her ears. "Just be glad there 's no Meinee and Moe to make any more racket!"

Both parrots jumped to the floor and hopped up to Ginger and Alice. "Let's play tag! You're it!" they screamed.

The next instant they flew straight upward and dropped

back to the floor just behind Ginger and Alice. "You'll never catch us!" they shrieked.

The two gerbils spun around, but Eenee and Meenee were in the air again, fluttering just above their heads.

"These feathered flea brains have to be grounded," growled Alice, swiping at both birds.

"This is five times worse than pulling Billy's truck around with my tail," groaned Ginger. "Don't Eenee and Meenee know any better games?"

"You're tired of tag?" the two parrots chirped as they buzzed past Ginger's ear. "Then let's play dive bomber!" In an instant they were flying back and forth close to the ceiling, squawking commands. "Two enemy battleships below! Prepare to attack!"

"I have a funny feeling we're the battleships," Ginger exclaimed. "What'll we do?"

"I don't know about you, but I'm not about to be sunk by those pint-sized pilots," Alice replied as she scrambled beneath the coffee table.

Ginger saw two green and yellow streaks swooping down toward her. She closed her eyes, ducked, and felt two pairs of wing tips brush her head. "Enemy ship hit but not sunk!" cried both birds.

Eenee and Meenee zipped back toward the ceiling then dove again at Ginger. A second before they reached her, she scurried under the table with Alice. "Those guys are really crazy!" she panted.

Alice gritted her teeth. "I'm surprised it took you so long to notice! We definitely have to do something about those pesky doofs, but I'm not sure what. Any suggestions?"

"Don't ask me!" Ginger complained. "Aren't you the one

who always has everything figured out?" Before Alice could answer, Mrs. Franklin called to her and Ginger. "Hey, you guys! Come out of there!"

The two gerbils poked their heads out from beneath the coffee table and looked around cautiously. Mrs. Franklin was sitting on the floor in the middle of the room. Eenee and Meenee had landed on Billy's tinker-toy ferris wheel, panting with exhaustion.

"You guys really must have had fun," Mrs. Franklin chuckled. "You gave Eenee and Meenee quite a workout! I can tell the four of you really like each other. Try not to be too hard on your new friends, though. They're not used to a lot of rough housing."

"I can't believe she said that," muttered Alice. "She thinks **we** gave **them** a workout! I can tell we've got quite a week ahead of us."

<h1 style="text-align:center">CHAPTER 6</h1>

It was, indeed, quite a week. Ginger and Alice had almost no rest. Whenever Billy took them out of their container, Eenee and Meenee were waiting, eager to play nerve-wracking games.

At first the two birds were rambunctious but good natured, but soon they turned nasty. Three days after dive bombing Ginger, they insisted on playing monopoly. They played poorly, then became furious when Alice and Ginger won every game. Soon play money and instruction cards were flying in all directions, and ear-splitting screams filled the air.

"Those guys are sure sore losers," Ginger complained as the monopoly board sailed over her head.

"They're going to be even sorer when I get through with them!" shouted Alice above the uproar. "I'm going to give them something to squawk about!"

"Don't do anything foolish," Ginger cautioned. "Just be patient for four more days and our week with Eenee and Meenee will be over."

Alice pounded on the floor in frustration. "I'm afraid I'll be completely loony by then! Just think of it. The world's greatest mischief maker driven crazy by a pair of pipsqueak parrots!"

"You can stand it," said Ginger with a sly grin. "Remember what you told me about experts doing their best under pressure? In just a few more days you can look back at this week and say, 'I overcame the greatest challenge any mischief maker ever faced.' You'll also have a wonderful story to tell your grand children some day."

Alice looked at Ginger suspiciously. "You aren't making

fun of me, are you? Sometimes I get the feeling you don't appreciate my talents, even though you tell me how great I am."

"Oh, I appreciate your talents," replied Ginger, trying not to smile. "In fact, I understand you better than you understand yourself."

Alice wiped the corner of her eye. When she spoke, her voice trembled slightly. "You don't know how good those words make me feel!" she exclaimed. "I needed a good pep talk to raise my spirits. Now just let those little twits try to upset me. I'm ready for them!"

Eenee and Meenee tested Alice's patience the very next morning by challenging her and Ginger to a singing contest. Alice started with "Tiptoe Through the Tulips," and Ginger followed with "Row, Row, Row Your Boat."

"We've never heard anything so awful!" shrieked Eenee and Meenee, rolling on the floor with delight. "You guys sound like a couple of cats with their fur on fire."

"Let's hear you do better!" growled Alice, barely resisting

the urge to grab and pull feathers.

The two birds put their heads close together, whispered for a few seconds, then announced they would sing "When the Red, Red Robin Comes Bob, Bob, Bobbing Along." Taking a deep breath, they screamed, squawked, chattered and chirped for five minutes.

Alice's ears were ringing and her nerves were nearly frazzled, but she spoke calmly. "That was a fine song – if you like something that sounds like two crazy magpies yowling."

Alice's words sent Eenee and Meenee into a terrible tantrum. They leaped up and down, beat their wings against the floor, and squalled themselves hoarse. Then they flew madly back and forth just above the two gerbils' heads. As Ginger and Alice watched from beneath the coffee table, both birds swooped, darted, twisted, tumbled and performed dozens of crazy mid-air acrobatics.

"What in the world is going on in here?" exclaimed Mrs. Franklin, hurrying into the room.

"It's Eenee and Meenee" answered Billy, who was lying on the sofa trying to read a comic book. "I don't think it was a good idea to get them, Mom. All they do is make a racket and act screwy."

Mrs. Franklin ducked as Eenee and Meenee whizzed past her head. "Things would be a lot more peaceful around here without them," she admitted. "But I'm afraid Alice and Ginger would miss their new friends."

Alice scrambled out from beneath the table and dashed toward Mrs. Franklin. "No! No!" she shouted. "We can't stand those little twerps. Get rid of them!"

"Be careful, Alice. You're chained to the table!" shouted Ginger. At that instant Alice reached the end of her chain and was jerked sharply backwards. Her feet flew out from under her and she landed with an "Ooof" flat on her back.

Mrs. Franklin looked puzzled. "Why do you suppose Alice is so upset?" she asked Billy.

Billy shrugged his shoulders and said, "I have no idea. But she sure was squeaking. Wouldn't it be nice if people could understand gerbil talk?"

Ginger helped Alice to her feet. She could see her friend was groggy but not seriously injured. "You'll be fine in a minute or two," she assured Alice.

"No, I won't be fine until the Franklins realize what little monsters Eenee and Meenee are," wheezed Alice. "I'll have to show them when I make super mischief."

Ginger scratched her head and asked, "What will you do to Eenee and Meenee?"

Alice rolled her eyes, sighed, and said, "Oh, boy! Here we go again. Every time I come up with a really neat plan, you have no idea what it is. I'm getting tired of explaining."

"I don't mean to upset any one," Ginger apologized. "It's just that some of your plans are pretty strange. I never know whether they'll be simple and sensible or complicated and weird."

"Well, this plan's perfectly logical," Alice declared. "What I do to those feathered freaks will be my first super-mischief trick when I get rid of my vest and chain. It'll be really simple, too, because I'll only need a little piece of string."

Before Ginger could reply, Alice held up her paw. "Yon don't have to ask where the string will come from. I'll use the piece that's attached to Billy's toy truck – the piece he ties to your tail when you pull that dumb little thing around."

Ginger didn't think Alice's plan was wise, but she couldn't help smiling. "I'm not sure how you'll use the string," she replied. "But I know Eenie and Meenie won't be very happy when you get through with them."

Ginger and Alice were talking beside Billy's ferris wheel, where Eeenie and Meenie were perched. They would have known that trouble was ahead if they'd been listening. Instead, they were sleeping, with their heads tucked under their wings.

CHAPTER 7

Ginger was amused by Alice's plan to create problems for Eenee and Meenee. However, she wished Alice would forget about playing tricks on the Franklins. She was afraid Alice would get into really serious trouble. She also felt sorry for Billy and his mother because they had done their best to help Alice learn to behave.

Ginger felt even worse when she overheard Billy and his mother and father talking near the container on the night before they planned to set Ginger and Alice free from their vests and chains.

Ginger had been sleeping in the mansion with Alice and had been awakened by Mrs. Franklin's voice. "I think our gerbils deserve a big reward for being so good," she said. "They've played so well with Billy, and they've certainly been patient with Eenee and Meenee."

"What should we do for them?" asked Mr. Franklin. "I'm not sure exactly," Mrs. Franklin answered. "What do you think, Billy?"

Billy said he'd like to have a party with ice cream, soda pop, fancy hats and noise makers. "That would really make Ginger and Alice happy!" he exclaimed.

"Sounds fine to me," said Mr. Franklin. "I can buy all that stuff on my way home from work tomorrow afternoon. We can celebrate right after supper."

Mrs. Franklin said she'd make a big cake decorated with frosting, squash seeds, peanuts and pecans. "But let's keep the party a secret," she suggested. "It'll be fun to see how surprised Ginger and Alice are!"

"Should we wait until the party to take off their vests and chains?" Billy asked.

Mrs. Franklin thought for a second and then said, "No. We'll let Alice and Ginger loose early tomorrow morning, but we won't tell them about the party. It'll be the perfect end to a perfect day."

Ginger wondered what to do. She couldn't warn the Franklins that Alice was planning mischief because they wouldn't understand her squeaking. However, she didn't want the Franklins to arrange the party and then have to cancel it because Alice had misbehaved. "I'll just have to persuade Alice to act right," Ginger told herself. "And I'll have to work fast or she'll start playing her tricks as soon as the Franklins turn her loose!"

Ginger went to work on Alice as soon as she woke up in the morning. "Wouldn't you feel bad if you made someone very unhappy and then found out they'd been planning to do something really nice for you?" she asked.

Alice rubbed the sleep from her eyes, then yawned and scratched the top of her head. "How can you expect me to answer a question like that before breakfast?" she mumbled, heading for the seed bowl.

"I can't wait!" exclaimed Ginger. "We have to talk right now!"

"OK, OK," muttered Alice. "But make it quick! I'm so hungry my stomach's roaring and turning flip-flops."

"I'll get right to the point," said Ginger. "The Franklins will set us free this morning, then have a big party tonight to thank us for being good. You'll ruin everything if you make mischief. They've done so much for us, and it would be really mean to play tricks on them now."

Alice looked surprised. For a moment she also seemed confused. "You're sure the Franklins are giving us a big party?"

"I overheard them talking about it last night while you were asleep," Ginger replied.

Alice looked at Ginger suspiciously. "Did they say what we'd have to eat?"

"Ice cream and soda pop," answered Ginger. She could see that Alice was tempted. "Mrs. Franklin's even baking a special cake."

"Now my stomach's really roaring!" exclaimed Alice. "It would be a terrible shame to let all that yummy food go to waste."

"Then you'll behave?" asked Ginger, hoping Alice would be sensible.

Alice frowned and said, "Don't rush me! I have to eat breakfast before I decide."

Alice gobbled all of the seeds in the bowl. Then she began pacing back and forth on the porch of her mansion. She stroked her chin and mumbled to herself. Soon she was so deep in thought that she walked from one end of the container to the other without realizing where she was going.

Just as Alice was about to bump into the exercise wheel, Ginger turned her around and headed her back toward the mansion. When she was halfway there, she stopped suddenly. "I'm going to make the Franklins happy!" she declared.

"Whoopee!" shouted Ginger. "You've made the right choice. I know you had your heart set on super mischief, but you'll never be sorry you decided to behave!"

Alice looked puzzled. "Who said I'm going to behave?"

"You did!" shouted Ginger. "You just told me you'd make the Franklins happy. You can't do that by playing crazy tricks on them!"

"Maybe I should explain," replied Alice, looking rather smug. "I've just done some heavy thinking, and I'm not surprised you couldn't keep up with me."

"You mean you've just had another one of your weird brain storms," said Ginger, totally upset. "I don't want to hear what you're planning to do!"

Alice ignored Ginger's frustration. "The best thing I can do is create the greatest mischief that any gerbil has ever made," she declared. "I know that sounds a bit off-the-wall, but look at it this way: I'll become world famous, and Billy and his family will become famous, too. Newspapers and TV reporters will do stories about them. The Franklins might even get rich by writing their own book about me! That would make them a lot happier than if I decided to behave."

Ginger was so shocked she couldn't speak for several seconds. "You're completely whacky!" she finally exclaimed.

"Not at all," replied Alice. "If you really think about what I've just told you, you'll realize I'm right. It may take you a while to understand. Until then you'll just have to trust me."

CHAPTER 8

Ginger had no intention of trusting Alice. She was sure she was headed for disaster, and she only hoped she could keep her from wrecking the Franklins' house. But before Ginger could think of a plan, Billy appeared and said, "Good news, guys! You don't have to wear your vests and chains any more! From now on you can go anywhere in the house. You're free!"

Mrs. Franklin was standing beside Billy. "We're really proud of the way you two have behaved," she said as Billy lifted Ginger and Alice from the container and set them on the floor.

It took the gerbils several minutes to get used to their new freedom. Ginger felt her stomach and back three times to make sure her vest was gone. Alice was so happy she dashed toward the middle of the room. She stopped suddenly, however, thinking she might still be chained to the coffee table.

Billy watched his pets for a few minutes. Then he went into his bedroom to check on a hundred grasshoppers he was keeping in a box for a school science project. Mrs. Franklin disappeared into the kitchen and began rattling pots and pans.

"She's making our party cake," Ginger told Alice. "Too bad we won't be eating it!" Alice was looking at Eenee and Meenee, who were climbing up and down Billy's ferris wheel. "How can I think about a cake when our feathered friends need someone to play with?" she asked with a sly smile.

As Ginger watched, Alice challenged the two parrots to a race. "I can run five times back and forth across this room before you guys can fly across it once!" she declared.

"You can't be serious," sneered both birds in perfect harmony. "We can fly five times faster than you can run!"

"Then let's see you do it," said Alice. "We'll start right here beside the coffee table. When I say 'Go,' we'll be off."

Alice and Eenee and Meenee lined up, Alice said "Go," and the race began. It was no contest. Before Alice was half way across the room, both birds had flown back and forth four times. "How could you think you'd win?" they snickered as they zipped past her.

"I'm not as smart as you guys," shouted Alice, telling a fib that the two birds were sure to believe. She was also running quite slowly to save energy.

Eenee and Meenee were laughing too hard to notice. They flew as fast as they could to make Alice look as foolish as possible. Soon they were so weary they were barely able to flutter back to the ferris wheel.

"We really showed that dumb gerbil!" Meenee panted. "That's for sure," wheezed Eenee. "By now she ought to know she can't get the best of us!"

The two parrots would have continued their conversation, but they quickly fell asleep. As they nodded off, Alice removed the string from Billy's toy truck and tied one end to each of their tails. Then she pushed the ferris wheel over. "You guys may be bushed, but I bet you'll have plenty of pep to play this game," she laughed.

The wheel crashed to the floor, sending tinker toys flying in all directions. Eenee and Meenee weren't hurt, but they were badly frightened. And as they fell, they discovered they were pulling each other down.

"Let go of my tail!" screamed Eenee. "What are you talking about?" Meenee squalled. "You're holding on to mine!"

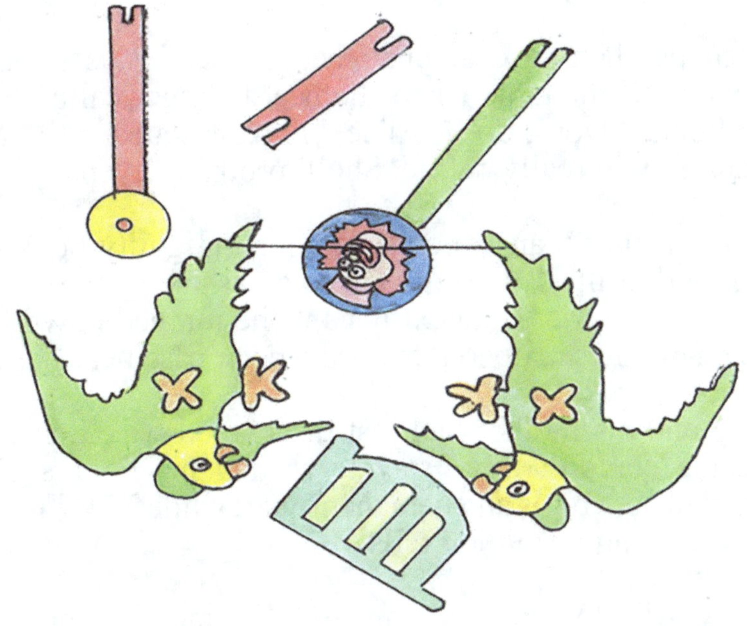

The two birds rolled around in the middle of the shattered ferris wheel, shrieking at the top of their lungs.

"Good heavens!" cried Mrs. Franklin, looking in from the kitchen. "Billy! Come quick! There's something wrong with Eenee and Meenee."

As soon as Billy saw the two thrashing parrots, he tried to pick them up. "Owwwww!" he yelled, jerking his hand back. "Those little busters bite!"

While Billy and Mrs. Franklin were wondering what was wrong, Alice was scampering toward Mr. Franklin's big easy chair, ready for super mischief. Leaping and clawing, she scrambled up the side of the chair and jumped onto the table where Mrs. Franklin's favorite vase was standing.

"I should've climbed the chair the first time we tried to break that dumb piece of glass," she told herself. "Trying to pull it down from the floor was stupid!"

Alice put her nose against the vase and was about to shove it off the table when she heard Ginger calling from the floor. "Don't do it, Alice," Ginger squeaked. "Mrs. Franklin will really be sad. She'll probably even cry!"

"Oh, all right!" answered Alice, feeling guilty but trying to sound gruff. "Who'd want to smash such an ugly old thing anyway?" The next instant she jumped down from the chair and scampered toward a book case near the TV.

Billy and his mother had just discovered why Eenie and Meenie couldn't fly. Bravely risking his fingers, Billy grabbed both birds and held them apart while Mrs. Franklin cut the string from their tails.

"Only Alice would pull an awful stunt like this," she exclaimed, sounding angry and disappointed. "Now where do you suppose she went?"

Billy scanned the room. "I don't see that fat old mischief maker," he answered. "But here's Ginger jumping up and down on the floor beside us."

"Alice is up there," squeaked Ginger, waving toward the top of the book case.

The Franklins had no idea what Ginger was squeaking about, but they looked in the direction she was pointing. Billy said, "If I didn't know better, I'd think she's telling us there's something wrong with our big ivy plant on the book case."

"There is something wrong!" shouted Mrs. Franklin. "The ivy's falling to pieces!" "That's Alice," cried Ginger, still jumping up and down, trying to make herself understood. "She's chewing off the branches of the ivy!"

Mrs. Franklin rushed toward the ivy just as the last branch fell off. Then she saw Alice hanging over the edge of the book case, ready to drop to the floor. "Eeeech!" she screamed. "I'll wring that rascal's neck when I get my hands on her."

There was no chance to catch Alice because she had dashed out of the living room toward the bathroom and bedrooms. Billy searched the bathroom but found no trace of her. Next, he hurried into his parents' bedroom and looked under the bed and dressers. He even opened the closet and pushed aside twenty pairs of shoes.

Suddenly he heard a bang and thump in his bedroom. Dashing through the door, he almost stepped on Alice as she scampered back toward the living room.

One glance told Billy what had happened. "Mom!" he shouted. "That little monster pushed my grasshopper collection off my desk. The lid's off the box, and there's grasshoppers everywhere – even on the ceiling!"

Mrs. Franklin was in such a hurry to help Billy inspect the damage that she failed to notice Alice darting into the kitchen. Ginger saw her, however, and tried to head her off. "You've played enough tricks!" Ginger exclaimed. "The Franklins are so angry that there's no telling how they'll punish you!"

Alice skidded to a stop in front of the refrigerator. Spinning around, she shouted "Squealer! Why did you let Billy and his mother know I was chewing up the ivy plant? It was delicious. If you hadn't interfered, I would have eaten all the evidence."

"I was only trying to keep you from getting into really bad trouble," replied Ginger. "I'm the best friend you have, even if you don't know it."

Alice was so angry she could hardly stand still. "I don't believe a word you say!" she snapped. "Now let me alone so I can play my best super trick!"

Alice whirled and leaped up on a drawer Mrs. Franklin had opened when she started making her cake. After jumping to two other open drawers, Alice hopped up on the kitchen counter beside the sink and looked around.

On one side of the sink sat a glass-measuring cup and a box of cake mix. A large bowl filled with batter stood on the other side. Directly above the bowl, high on the wall, was a shelf that held three huge china plates and an electric clock. The cord of the clock hung down the wall and was plugged into an outlet a few inches above the counter. Alice grabbed the cord and began climbing.

After several seconds, she clambered onto the shelf. Then, as Ginger watched from the floor far below, Alice started testing the plates to see how heavy they were.

"Oh, no! She's going to knock them off!" cried Ginger. "The Franklins will kill her for sure!"

Alice quickly realized she'd have trouble moving the plates because they were heavy and stood on edge in a groove that ran the length of the shelf. To make matters worse, there wasn't enough space between the plates and the wall, so Alice couldn't push them from behind.

"Sheesh!" she growled. "Being the world's greatest mischief maker can be a real problem!"

Alice grabbed the edge of the middle plate and tried to pull it forward. The plate wouldn't budge, so she pulled harder.

Suddenly her feet slipped and she tumbled backward off the shelf.

Turning a complete somersault, she landed with a **SPLASH** in the bowl of batter.

"This is ridiculous," Alice muttered as she tried to pull herself out of the sticky cake mix. The sides of the bowl were slippery, and the more she struggled, the deeper she sank into the batter. It began running into her mouth and nose, and suddenly she realized she might drown.

"Help! Someone get me out of here!" she gasped.

CHAPTER 9

As soon as Alice fell from the shelf, Ginger scrambled up the open drawers to the counter to try to help her. She grasped the rim of the bowl and pulled herself up until she could look down at the batter. Only the top of Alice's head was visible. Ginger pulled herself higher, leaned over the rim, and called to her unlucky friend.

"I'm here, Alice. Can you reach up to me?"

Alice said something that sounded like "blub, blub, blub" and stuck her paw out of the batter. Ginger grabbed it and pulled. Soon Alice's whole head emerged. "I'm a goner if I go under again!" she sputtered. "I can hardly breathe now."

"Don't worry. I've got you!" Ginger replied.

Ginger pulled harder, but Alice's paw was so slippery she lost her grip. Alice began sinking, and in a few seconds she would disappear completely.

Ginger tried to stay calm. She knew she couldn't pull Alice from the bowl, but she hoped Billy or Mrs. Franklin could save her. "They're probably still in Billy's bedroom catching grasshoppers," Ginger told herself. "I've got to get them out here!"

Ginger thought about climbing down to the floor and running into the bedroom, but she quickly realized Billy and his mother wouldn't know what she wanted. Even if she could make the Franklins understand that Alice needed help, they probably wouldn't reach the kitchen in time.

Suddenly a really weird idea popped into her head. "Wouldn't it be crazy if I helped rescue Alice by using her own kind of super mischief?" she thought.

"I'll behave just like Alice!" Ginger decided and ran to the measuring cup that Mrs. Franklin had left near the sink. She shoved the cup off the counter top and heard it shatter as it hit the floor.

"Wouldn't you know it! Alice is playing more tricks!" shouted an angry voice from beyond the living room.

A few seconds later Billy dashed into the kitchen and looked at the floor. "Broken glass!" he shouted. "Wait until I get my hands on that furry little pain-in-the-neck!"

Suddenly Billy saw Ginger on the counter top jumping up and down and waving. "What the heck's going on?" he asked, "Why are you squeaking and pointing at the mixing bowl?"

Billy glanced into the bowl but saw nothing unusual. "Big deal!" he said. "That's Mom's cake batter. What do you want me to do with it, Ginger? Put it into the oven?"

The thought of Billy baking Alice terrified Ginger. "Alice is in the batter! Please get her out!" she squeaked at the top of her lungs.

Billy looked down into the bowl again. This time he saw something really strange. "Hey! There's a tail sticking out!" he shouted.

It took Billy only a second to pull Alice out of the batter. "Oh, no!" he screamed. "Mom! Alice is dead!"

"What happened?" gasped Mrs. Franklin, bursting into the kitchen.

Billy laid Alice on the counter and began to cry. "Somehow

she fell into your cake mix and couldn't get out!" he sobbed. "It's all my fault! If I had tried to catch her after she ran out of my bedroom, she'd still be alive. I was more worried about those stupid grasshoppers than about my favorite pet!"

Mrs. Franklin put her arms around Billy and told him no one was to blame. "We had no way of knowing Alice would run wild when we took off her vest and chain," she said. "She was just a mischievous gerbil who got into trouble once too often."

"But she was so cute, and I'm really going to miss her," moaned Billy.

"I know," Mrs. Franklin replied. "I feel just as bad as you do, but things could be worse. We'll have to get rid of Eenee and Meenee because they bite and use terrible language, but we'll still have Ginger. I know she can't replace Alice, but she's a fine pet."

"If Alice was alive, I'd forgive her for all the tricks she's played on us!" Billy sniffed. "She is alive!" shouted Mrs. Franklin. "She just moved her head!"

Billy grabbed a towel and wiped Alice's face. "I can't believe it! She's opening her eyes," he shouted. "Yippee! She's a gooey, sticky, drippy mess, but I think she's going to be OK."

Alice sat up, looked around, and said, "What's going on? How'd I get out of that gooey, sticky, drippy stuff?"

"Billy pulled you out!" exclaimed Ginger, who was overjoyed that Alice had survived. "He saved your life!"

"But how'd Billy know I needed to be saved?" Alice wondered. "I gave him the slip after I dumped out his grasshoppers. He had no idea I was in the kitchen."

Ginger smiled slyly and said, "Some other super-mischief maker played a trick that got his attention and rescued you. That's all I'm going to tell you."

"Well, I don't want to meet whoever did that because I'm through with super mischief!" Alice declared.

"You need a bath, Alice" said Mrs. Franklin. "Then after supper we'll have a party. You really don't deserve one, and we can't have the cake because you've ruined the batter. But you're alive and well, and that's an excellent reason to celebrate."

Mrs. Franklin filled the kitchen sink with warm water, added sudsy soap, and scrubbed Alice clean with a big soft-bristled brush.

"This is almost as ridiculous as wearing a vest and chain," muttered Alice as she stretched to keep her head above water. **"But I really don't mind!"**

We Hope You Enjoyed Our Story!